Expresslanes Through the Inevitable City

R. Craig Sautter

**Photographs
Dennis Wiss**

**December Press
Highland Park, Illinois**

A special issue of December Magazine,
comprising vol. 33, nos. 1–2, 1990

Expresslanes Through the Inevitable City by R. Craig Sautter

ISBN: 0-913204-26-9
Library of Congress Catalog Card Number: 90-83148

Manufactured in the United States of America

Published by December Press
Box 302, Highland Park, Illinois 60035

For Sally

Special thanks to Dr. Richard J. Curtis

Now, what is poetry?
If you say, "it is simply words,"
I will say, "a good poet gets rid of words."
If you say, "it is simply meaning,"
I will say, "a good poet gets rid of meaning."
But you say, "If words and meaning are gotten rid of,
      where is the poetry?"
To this I reply, "Get rid of words and meaning,
      and there is still poetry."

                Yang Wan-li
                (1127–1206)

Some of these poems have appeared in *Assembling, Central Park, The Green Fuse, Indigo, The Madison Review, MC, The Midway Review, Road Apple Review, The Third Eye, Velvet Wings* and have been displayed at The Pratt Graphics Center.

Contents

State of the Union

Silver streams of sonic jets settle down into
Newark's toxic necropolis pulsating in diesel heat,
scientific sun-runners remotely patterned
by silicon passenger system from runway to runway.
New Jersey rising up angry against the noxious
petroleum sludge fatally poisoning New York Harbor.
Their rivalry is geo-corporately political.
Out of the exhaust-pipe dreams of under-river tunnels,
trucks and cars back into the Exxon swamplands,
fast-food festivals, marauding mini-malls,
paved patriotic prairies, into the buffaloless range
round-ups of ranchyard homes with beat-'em-up cowboys.
Its sky sewn together with stitches of telephone wire,
its soul electrocuted with TV antennas.
Make our way back across this minefield without injury
and we become the payrolled ministers of suc-cess,
con-artists of con-quest, mass-marketable mannequins
of power, greed and cash-on-credit-card installments.
Those with light injuries run our schools, our factories,
our insurance schemes, our soundtracks, our lives.
Poets go mute with numbers, poets go blind.
When it is hardly night and air conditioners moan,
the skeptical moongazer takes a second look.
America becomes an hap-hazardous diversion for long-departed
contemporary Galileo peering back through convex glass.
Doesn't he know the demented doctor about to perform
lobotomy is only our Marcus Welby?

1

Passenger

There she sat
old and admitting it.
Suitcase wedged between her feet
black hands clasped in
that calm, respectful position
eyes bewildered
dodging glances
broad-rimmed straw hats incite.
"In the ghetto it is still 1930."
What can she make of it?
All her life trained
to miss the stern white stare,
now even having to avoid
the young explosive black one.
It is not easy to forget,
Marcus Garvey had his day,
now almost impossible to hope,
riding this subway apartment
South and North and West and East
another sleepless night of fear.
An ebony buddha of suffering?
Again leaden metal doors
screech open and shut,
who knows what streets appear
at the end of these tunnels?
She pulls unmatched gloves
from her burlap purse,
tightens her long scarf
of throwaway lace,
momentarily traps her icy replica
in green glass succession
of passing traincars
and proudly smiles at me with
her calm exhausted reply,
"Yes, child, but I have survived."

Mainstreamed

Buddy's a week out of Bellevue
and already he wants to jump the Brooklyn Bridge
into water harder than Atlantic Avenue
because no one buys old leather shoes he sells
next to the IRT stairwell on 14th Street.
The East River would cure his nerves but crush
his braincells and feed his bone marrow
to the cockroaches on Ellis Island.
From there Buddy tells us he thinks
he could join a chorus of circling seagulls.
Maybe he's right. We decide to follow.

In the First Years of Peace

The dead Asians are downtown Manhattan
occupying all the seats at the breakfast counter.
It pisses us off for those yellow jokers
to beat us to the scrambled eggs,
they not having to be in the office selling shares by 9 a.m.
and besides, what the hell are they doing here anyway,
now that the war is over?

The Late American Sonnet

What is the I the I the I the I?
O What is I is I is I is I?
What is the I the I the I the I?

Where is the I the I the I the I?
O Where is I is I is I is I?
Where is the I the I the I the I?

When is the I the I the I the I?
O When is I is I is I is I?
When is the I the I the I the I?

Who is the I the I the I the I?
O Who is I is I is I is I?
Who is the I the I the I the I?

O Why is I is I is I is I?
O Why is I is I is I is I?

The Poet

I have given childhood too many chances,
now I exhale blood-specked ash
and slip unresistingly into a hard steel chair.

My dreams drown with death masks dripping,
when I wake there is no sound of thunder.
I scale angry dry skies at dusk,
yet there is no sign of static rage.

My memories stray through chaffed rows
of summer wheat ripe before the roar,
menacing blackbirds hover in the woozy calm.

On afternoons bloated by humidity-swollen skin,
I finger flaxen pages of aged photographs,
stacks of negatives disintegrate at my touch.

Swarming flies infect the tongues of honeysuckle,
their sunless seeds wither in larva beds,
nothing follows August.

I fold with exhaustion of too many recollections,
thoughts slump like petrified stone pulse,
words stiffen into unconnected syllables.

Now the poetic annihilation begins.

The Inevitable City

He has moved to the new city,
lived there alone,
watching the city change
him.
Without resistance it comes,
since it is not change
of good
            or evil.

He begins to wonder
what change is,
knowing even that it will
not matter what is changed.

His vision wanders off
with smoke escaping sunset.
Summer again.

The heat increases with
the hours on August 6th.

He thinks of other cities,
of where cities dissolve.

A word from the radio
sets him in dizzy turmoil.

His face glows.

He hears nothing in the heat.

He comes to where
his sight leaves him.
He comes to where
he can no longer walk,
to where others dare

not to bother him.
He comes to the edge
of the inevitable city,
where the city beyond change
opens to him,
comes to where the buildings
are evacuated,
turned to rubble.

The fields are feverish with
citizens who can no longer
recognize him.
Who scream when he comes.
Band together into
a single group,
pick rocks from decayed buildings.

Smash his skull
and kick until
the sound leaves his body.

He comes to where death
squeals like a newborn child,
to where an old man's voice
fills the city like a siren.

On Eighth Avenue

"Excuse
my
intrusion,"

bum
but
cigar
parting
parched
lips
his
smile
euphoric,

"but
all
energy
is
ultimately
light,

got
a
match?"

The Philosopher

"I used to think,
                    therefore,
I probably was."

The Common Man

The common man asks himself why he is so frightened,
The common man asks himself why he is so poor,
The common man asks himself why he feels so alone,
The common man knows his questions will remain unanswered.
The common man need not ask why he is so addicted to TV.

Uptown A

                    disbursing these expenditures with caution.
          a hot dog and coffee with a token's chance at success.
               because this man and then this woman are vanishing
          like light bulbs
                         popping on the A-Train
                    when it rounds the curve into Times Square.
          all you 72nd-street junkies out.
                    all you queens and salesmen too.
                    this here's the Harlem Special!

125th Street Blues

I want to talk about the childhood I never had,
Couldn't find the good underneath the bad,
Never had a home where I could lay my head,
Took all of my power just to keep myself fed.

Coppers would bust us wherever we would meet,
That was just a part of living off the streets,
Spent most of my teens trying to keep from dying,
Couldn't find no job, no use in trying.

Hot summer nights with nothing to do,
Hot city nights when I first meet you,
You were the first one ever to show me love,
I was the first one to ever give you some.

Now I don't know why it all went wrong,
We were burning with a love so sure and strong,
But your father said I wasn't your kind of man,
Your brother called me down so I took my stand.

Talk to me, baby, if you understand,
Talk about our life in this promised land,
Because from my position it don't look too good,
Everybody starving in these gutted neighborhoods.

Before I knew it there were cops on the scene,
Someone fired a bullet and I heard you scream,
I lunged out, girl, to stop you from falling,
Through breaking glass my name you were calling.

I swear to you, baby, I never fired a shot,
I swear to you, baby, from the bottom of my heart,
But before you were cold, I was beaten in this jail,
Couldn't find no judge who would throw my bail.

10

Talk to me, baby, in the cold moon light,
Talk to me, baby, I'm dying of fright,
Send me a kiss on these midnight clouds,
I'll be with you, child, in a few more hours.

Was it your brother who fired those shots?
Was it police waiting with some twisted plot?
No one listened when I took the witness stand,
Just another poor scapegoat in this legal land.

So talk to me, baby, if you understand,
Tell me about our life in some distant land,
You offered me love like a fresh-water well,
But it fades so fast in this death row cell.

Indictment

Now there are lots of coppers
in this great big land,

Lots of coppers grabbing with
their copper hands,

Lots of prosecutors crying
for the first degree,

Lots of lawyers crawling
for their lawyering fee.

But ain't it a crime when people
got nothing to eat?

When it's 10 below zero
and they're living on the streets?

Ain't it a crime
when they can't find a job?

When banks run the cities
like a '30s mob?

Ain't it a crime that billions
on war are spent?

Ain't it a crime we ain't civilized yet?

After Eden
(A psycholinguistic historical explanation of social behavior)

Man: noun, male, gentleman, sir, master, yeoman, chap, swain, fellow, blade, beau, husband, youth, mister, Mr., monsieur, herr, signore, senor, senhor, cock, drake, gander, dog, boar, stag, hart, buck, stallion, gelding, tom, adj. masculine, manly, virile, unwomanly, unfeminine.

Woman: noun, female, petticoat, womankind, womanhood, the Sex, fair sex (as opposed to unfair sex), softer sex, dame, madam, lady, donna, belle, matron, dowager, girl, youth, mistress, Mrs., Miss, Ms., madame, frau, signore, senora, senhora, tame cat, hen, bitch, slut, sow, doe, roe, mare, she-goat, nanny, ewe, cow, lioness, tigress, vixen, harem, seraglio, purdah, adj. feline, womanly, lady-like, matronly, girlish, maidenly, womanish, effeminate, unmanly.

Night Mare

Your radar tracks infra-red excursions
through emerald night sanctuaries
where florescent swallow and embryonic minnow
wail with whirlpool spider eggs
behind your sulfur powdered eyes
cursed by a living I do not yet understand
while sea-horses gliding on red solar wings
spanning three hundred and fifty feet
guard the overgrown gates of your giant cage.
You scream
because you know escape is an illusion.
When you wake your face is already crumbling fossil.

13

The Crime

By putting on these gloves
I become anonymous in the house
of cool blue menthol lights.

By putting on these gloves
I exempt myself from examination
in the chambers of political faith.

By putting on these gloves
I break the path of causality which
links me to the transgression.

By putting on these gloves
I sketch an arrow in the dusty road
and take a Greyhound to Chicago
instead of Riker's Island.

By putting on these gloves
I beat the Macbeth complex, save
on Ivory soap, and am guaranteed
five to seven hours sleep a night.

By putting on these gloves
I let fly a mirage which lodges
in the space between
bedlamps at daybreak
and a NASA satellite's beam.

By putting on these gloves
I sign a pact with Genet
to buy the pool hall
on the corner of 46th Street and 10th Avenue
and to change the rhythm of stoplights
when no ambulances are available.

By putting on these gloves
I join the long lines
of financial hit-men
clogging the grand boulevards at midnight
paying off their victims' bankruptcies.

By putting on these gloves
I acknowledge the probability of suicide
before human compassion.

By putting on these gloves
I announce "A Crime is about to occur"
on a clock which vows
"It has already happened."

Rage

It's a deeper fog,
But you're coming back to sight,
Through the concrete-shattered glass,
That I empty out tonight.

Garcia Lorca

Garcia Lorca
this literary ignorance of mine
        gives me no pleasure.
I would gladly write this poem on your poems
but it is only the sound of your name
    —your Spanish squeal febrile
on the uptown Broadway tenement roof—

1937
War on the peninsula
your Latin territory scarred
fury of air raid whistles swell
storm of gasoline iron scraps.
These among your torments—
an exile with many hiding places
    yet only one destiny.

        Garcia
    Lorca—
who did you leave behind here?
Were your arms of resignation spread
like Goya's execution of 1808?
    It is important to see
        what peace here
        and war there
            have brought.

Upon whose heroism
        upon what martyr
should these tattered people who remain
    toss a coin of ineffable envy?

Garcia
    Lorca—
this poem has no determinacy to accuse
        you least of all

but here we still are
in peace
that is war
in hate that is
impoverished and terrified
of what you knew—
what is now known by all.

So it is Garcia
I utter your name
as a terrible question
pondering why you have gone
and who
is condemned
to follow.

Joint Communique
from and to the fiber-optic century

Beep: "Listen up, men—
   Beep: "We've got a tough chore ahead of us
         we can't start complaining now
                           or whining about *.*"

What is it?? Gee what could make mom and pop and the sarge and
the prez sooo excited at one time???

               "Sit down, kids—this will be hard
                                   to take . . .
         You see, things aren't exactly like . . .
            well, like we told ya
                        —things are a little scarier!"

"Another Century Speaks," beeps the super-vax
      telex from Chi-cag-oo.

"I know that I am in a city soon to be racked by hell,"
   she whispered,
            as though the lost sensations of this spring night
                     were her forbidden memory.

         She had been a girl then
      when her brother was executed by the Nationalist Guard
         for stealing bread from the ration storehouse
            for Central Manhattan
            42nd Street and Eighth Avenue.
                                 HARD PORN.

"Wake up, mom—
               It's only me and Lassie."
OOhh, Jeff*** I must
            have been ***"

               My uncle put his foot through our new TV
               I thought he was fucking crazy,

that was 1953
two years before the executive chamber
assembled contingency plans for suspending
elections
for "reasons" of National Insecurity.

The high-speed computer memory chip in New New York
remembers a genetic theory of some untamed poet reading
Schopenhauer in Bloomington Spring long ago, with florid
organic phosphorous formations spreading all around him,
reluctantly forecast that Hitler was not the culmination of
cultural atrocities but just the beginning . . .

because World War I bore more mutants than ever
before and that number was geotemporally multiplied
by World War II and that now the victorious war mutants
are in control with common codes
and advanced programs for the final offensive . . .

and that we . . .

we who read this desperate memory track
are only a colony of quarantined survivors
targeted for the last attack.

Searching for the displaced misinformation files on dulles/
macnamara/ nixon/ kissinger/ helms/ reagan/ bush
Request memory feeds on da nang
phnum penh
beirut
san salvador . . .
Request . . .
until the tone of the telex shifts codes
and that dead language is deleted.

There is a girl on this park bench crying.

I think she knows too.

Target

She is a target
wherever she walks
long dress or short
blonde hair or brunette
naked in bondage
to chronic fear that stalks her
inside this concrete urban cage
with two pink and white
bull's eyes
stamped on her blouse
where the passion
of every random psychopathological
predator pants
as she passes
through the tribunal of hungry streets.
Tied and gagged
and tormented
by their hate-infested gawk
long before their hands trespass
and tear at her buttons
slap at her face
slash at her arms with razors,
the violation threatens
wherever she strolls,
an assault that drags her across the open alleys
across the offices and the parking lots
across the carpets of entertainment dens,
an onslaught against her spirit
every time a man enters the room.
If she could kill she might sometime,
when their invasion comes
when their pathetic stares
turn loose their crusade for cordial skin
and she becomes a perishable produce
weeping in the wilderness of suffocating night

another statistic on some police blotter
one of the 4,054 rapes this year,
this city,
this slaughterhouse,
where every six minutes
a generation of women
are herded through this asylum of dread
and humiliation.

The Howler

The howler carries a disease
embedded deep in his skull,
a plague, a pestilence,
a hypodermic evacuation,
a ritual, a ceremony,
a plan of extinction
as wild as a pack of mad dogs
loose in the vacant lots and alleys
at the edge of town.
The howler
carries death
with his bite,
which he buries in your soft flesh
to the bone whose marrow
tastes like salty blood tonic.

Dreaming of Marina

Afterwards you toss all night beside me,
fatally tied to the dream that comes again as
that murder came along the avenue where last she walked
three months ago in the warm drizzle of August morning
when he struck steel against her neck and shoved her
to the pavement for the four dollars left in her purse
because he needed cash to fix brakes on his rusted car.
Bewildered, angry and broken-hearted, you will not let go
of your long talks over coffee or the unfinished phone calls
sometimes so fabulously animated, amiable and delightful,
sometimes so distraught, unreasonable and unresolved,
all gone now like pools of milk from a bottle shattered
on the curb where last she knew consciousness and terror.
You stutter in your sleep as you try to comfort her, tell her
not to surrender to the senselessness that surrounds us all,
that nothing else matters now but the tranquility she knows,
the peace beyond the world that no one here can find,
an eternal truce that so eluded her in this city of carnage
where she witnessed so much anguish, distress and poverty,
and worked to alleviate others' torment, before her own.
You whisper now to tell her she must fight it no more,
must yield to what is final, if not good, then perhaps
still causing some good in its unbearable aftermath,
in the way we remember her puzzled smile and reckless laugh,
in the way we live a little for her, for those she protected,
outside the nightmare where I cautiously shake you to let go.

The Prezidential Committee Reports

Violence comes to violence.
Now it comes to you.
What can we say?
Violence sweeps us all away.

Principles of Life Insurance

1) Someone Dies When You Collect
2) Someone Dies When You Collect
3) Someone Dies When You Collect
4) Someone Dies When You Collect
5) Someone Dies When You Collect
6) Someone Dies When You Collect
7) Someone Dies When You Collect
8) Someone Dies When You Collect
9) Someone Dies When You Collect
10) Someone Dies When You Collect
11) The Insurance Company Lives On

Sestina

Gone
    mad
   gone
       mad
      gone
       mad?

Mad.
  Gone
       gone
   mad
      mad?
          Gone?

Gone
  mad
    mad
      gone
        mad
          gone?

Gone
  gone
     mad
     mad
       gone
         mad?

Mad?
Mad?
Mad?
   Gone?
   Gone?
   Gone?

Gone mad.
Gone mad.
Gone mad.

Reform Movement

Kill,
　　what you
　　　　eat.

Eat,
　　what you
　　　　kill.

The Totally Lost Generation

Who said it was me or him or you who made history?
Walter was there and so were we and anyone with a TV.
Don't you remember anymore?
You got up and opened a refrigerator during the commercial
breakdown.
When you came back Ike, Kennedy, Johnson, Nixon, Ford,
Carter, Reagan and Bush
had all been branded with the President Seal
and Quayle was ready for combat flight?
But the icebox was empty except for two rotten eggs
and a gallon of sour milk,
and jeesss we missed all the real shows in between.
Even though "The Cold War was over,"
they talked about nuclear warheads
like they were picking mushroom tabs.
One morning the generals ate some magic buttons in New Mexico
and the sky turned purple
and their faces melted like molten black silver
and our fear vanished
into a silo of screams.
Somewhere beyond our bleeding planet
the television beam blared on and on.
Jeesss. I wish we could walk again.
Just to the corner liquor store some warm midnight
so I could buy a fifth to get us through.
Still, no one said it would be easy.
When you're making a profit that fast
you've got to expect some problems.
Besides, hysteria was on our side.
And there were more channels to flip on than ever.
But the commercials never ended
even when the planet did.
And though no one was smiling,
we were still selling toothpaste
on the solar system's network.

Curfew

Snow silence spills its truce onto the bombpocked intersection
   below.
Only moments ago she was among the five bodies soldiers
   dragged away.
Their lacerated doctrine of a just new age lacquered the cafe
   walls.
A severed heart of inconsolable solitudes is my last facade.
Everything I loved, extinguished in blasts of military rocketfire.
I am a broken wing wounded and abandoned on this hunted
   rooftop.
Government squads are scuffling across buildings around me.
This silence is a drumroll, a curfew broken with my single
   bullet.
I somersault through the gas-stained air she has already
   forgotten.
All I can remember of this life is her heart of sympathetic fury.

Vigil

These red lights
in the distant dark
have swallowed up
our tormented eyes
and the empty echo
of last night's bark
crushes silence upon
our tattered sighs
and this fantastic
repetition with its
ever-circling height
lunges at us
with vengeance
as we ask for peace
again tonight.

Nighthawking

Bayblow.
           Raw cold through these hands.

   Bars are closing in the Village.

  The echo I was hearing for years
      vanishes with steamed bodies
               piling into autos
  vacant in the night of subliminal suburbs.

  But I am serving my talent
               for dreams
  and fables
       on a Washington Square bench again.

Atman in Times Square

Where is that phone ringing?
On the desert island formed when Broadway intersects
Seventh Avenue
where shipwrecked and abandoned I have no alternative
except to answer the call that could be from anywhere
but when I pick up the hanging receiver in a chrome glass cave
a Hindi goddess announces her presence
on the other end of my weary consciousness
and commands me to fall to my knees and pray steadfastly
for the horde of forlorn refugees from every town and city
swarming around me like rabid black bats
homeless and hungry and eager for anything to fall to the ground
and screeching in a language I have never heard before
so obediently I shed my overcoat and give it to a barefoot woman
unfasten my watch for a blind dogless man
my tie I flip to the mad hatter dressed in an orange wool suit
I leave behind my shoes for a youngster who is shining his nickels
donate my pants for the rag man to fly on his grocery cart
stand imperially naked under the electronic news reel
where the names of South American torture victims
flash like jolts of electromagnetic voltage on organs of renewal
and picking up the receiver again for further instructions
hear nothing but a dial tone humming the World Spirit's
secret mantra
loud enough for all this city to hearken
pouring out of penthouses shedding their nobility
to enter our ecstacy
where we achieve Atman as easily as catching a cab downtown.

Southern Cross

Our century was left undiscovered,
   shapeless continental drifts
of fear, famine, plague, destruction,
   four pre-solar contortions
      of starmass and time
left waiting without distinction.

So on crackling urban evenings
   when anxiety exceeds even sorrow
the plea too shrill to be heard
   is your concealed confiscation of love.

Then whose mercy?
When this transplanetary mind breathes out
     moist ecstatic expectations
    spun on four poles of the universe,
   when it exhales
      the inflated sphere we inhabit?

Beneath the Southern Cross
   an agitated sea gives birth to an armada,
to a voyage beyond a last moment
         of discovery.

And overcome with our first encounter
      we prepare to re-name it all,
  with a language
   we have just begun
      to comprehend.

Heat Wave

Your voice enters my throat
               red with pleading.
Sanctuary walls
     scrapped of prehistoric paintings.
Somewhere in this predatory hunt
          staged in varnished apartments
     above the park,
   we inflate,
        float angry
               like helium proverbs.
And colliding with repeated punishment
     that is sorrow,
          even intuitions fail
        for uttering replies,
             for fingering sympathetic vowels.
So all afternoon you cry with the insects
   in the premature darkness.
Until we plunge again into scarlet silhouettes
     of the heat wave's residue,
Still too emotional
               for touching.

The Divorce

Their dissolution proved disastrous
leaving her with the imperialism of loneliness
conquering every emotion within her territory of grief
in the land of numbness
in the muted abode
there were no opportunities
to speak of anything
because her emptiness was deeper than silence
that could not be forgiven.
So she lived inside the newspaper walls she called her home
a still room with black telephone and ivory piano
playing a minuet of solitude
a ballad of despair
until another lover came
and another skirmish commenced.

Battery Park

At the edge of Battery Park
where sunset flesh New Jersey vents
gills in the heat wave
for wind to blow through,

Liberty salutes the oil boats,
gas tankers and Staten Island steambarges.

Before the monument of the dead
old black vets memorized names
of World War II brethren
inscribed on grey marble slabs.

The immigrants come down here to die.

Puerto Rican teens fantasize
the sex to come behind azalea bushes
when the moon wails out.

And sailors shipwrecked in '32
search the sports pages of the *Daily News*
but cannot recognize a hero.

Manhattan breathes out its tensions
and allows its brittle dried leaves
to absorb sea breeze.

Salt from mid-Atlantic decomposes
an industrial plague
making dreams easy.

Soon this sullen water swallows
what ranges beyond its shores
erases all mythical creatures
who crawled out on an invented earth.

Ocean inverts its hollow contemplation
and covers us over
cooling off the swelter
of the city's summer fever.

Silhouette

I saw your empty silhouette on the miles of fallow sand
when I walked there all alone
at the summer's tangled seaweed end.
The ring-billed gulls and nervous sandpipers seem to ask
"Where is her carcass thin and tanned?"
And I wonder quite the same of your smart and sensual fame.
Slouching near Wall Street for another gain?
Or browsing for jewels along Fifth Avenue?
For the cost of a cab
from the Bowery to the Cloisters
we could drink bourbon for a week
and live on blueberry pie or natural oysters.
So why have you ventured back
to run with the herd of that "cultured world,"
when ocean spray as pure as pearls
in saltwater smell and southerly sail
can be snatched so easily from the harbor's chest
in a single long and liberating breath?
For the first time in decades I will not return with you,
too many lessons here for me to renew,
instead I scratch these unanswered lines
in the silicon wash of September rhyme
thinking of our lost possibilities
when our former promises
take their leave
through the obsessive murmur of cooling autumn breeze.

Westbeth

Pastel sparks
graze her brush
hickory totem stripped of feathers
while in knitted mittens
and navy coat she composes
a gutterfill of November hues
collected outside her windowview
above Greenwich Avenue along the Hudson.
Too cold to snow.
Too cold to think.
Paint freezes and falls from her canvas.
Outside her dread of loneliness
lingers love.
Still, she counts the corpse
of drifting autumn leaves.
And shivers.

Jet Stream

Like an illumination of empyrean consciousness
this sleek system of steel force rises
35,000 feet above the slumbering globe and levels out
into a continuous serenity of cumulus white.

And at the horizon where we stare off through portals
into a turquoise-marine of inverted dream,
the stars light up in spite of the sun.

Inside our first-class compressurized compartment,
newspaper headlines of multi-national corporate affairs,
electronic commerce and junk-bonded industry,
make all this I see invisible.

I try to remember all the occasions of my solitude.
Not one will sell to these men of state.

Bughouse Square
1963

Cherry blend of slow coiled smoke filtered through October
evening on that first visit to the public square at Dearborn and
Delaware where ghosts of Dreiser, Dell and Debs defiantly
floated from stacks of the Newberry Library through autumn
corridors of fallen elm and locust leaves shredded under worn
leather soles of drifters and derelicts and discarded sages whose
soapbox orations resonated in crisp exhale with declarations so
strong they pulled a procession of boxcar veterans and
dispossessed parkbenchers who yet yearned for the poor man's
paradise, reciting a labor litany of their prophet Trotsky whose
dialectical laws of revolutionary praxis, economic justice,
international brotherhood and social art were still untaught to
white, barely 16-year-old, suburban nomads forever detoured
off the American expressways of success and status into the
city's uncontrollable desperation of destitution and hunger.

And then that first seductive hit of the sweet illicit seed passed
from hand to hand of black and white and brown teenaged
gangsters waiting for a midnight heist, watching crowds of
anxious faggots cowering near cruising intersections eluding
mancrushing cops while waving down their undercover lovers,
and the lines of antiquated homeless men, beaten senseless in
'30s steelyard strikes, jailed in '40s warcamps, exiled by '50s
blacklists, gathered again for utopian salvation amid the
groaning drunks who stumbled strung-out on piss-soaked dirt
walkways to mumble, cry and pray.

Still our confident expositions of ecstacy and existence, our
excursions through the city's shrill resistance transforming our
voyage of innocent words into the incessant memory of
exhausted faces peering through fifth-floor flophouse windows
filled with women the suburbs refused admission or remorse.

Devoured by it, compulsively returning for more drastic
debates staged against the jive saxophone moan blown wild
through the whirling autumn winds of our street-corner
verbal carnivals.

Then when winter sleet toppled those old men to their knees
begging for sleep while the hawkers enclosed for beatings,
our tongues still soared like snow in the arc of lamplights
illuminating a terror of syllables so resonant in their romance
of rage and rebellion.

Bughouse in the yellow haze of burning leaves and the
combustible awakening of unconventionalized
consciousness . . .

Bughouse in the shivering shelter of overcoats where blasts of
the northern hawk pressed our bodies around barrel-bellowed
bonfires held hard on abstracted arguments of the visionary
hooker . . .

Bughouse in the thaw of April, new season '64, with its
sorrowful parade of women also in their sixties but much more
tattered, and from the chess-playing seers, a tale of how in the
old days workingclass mothers strolled at dusk through the
park's cringing orange-red streaked sunsets given over now to
the migration of whores and useless white young . . .

Bughouse in the singe of summer, a congregated colony of
debaters constantly scattered by switchblade fights and
screaming blue cop cars stalking vagrant victims—
premonitions of how this all would be finally understood 30
blocks south in hot night shrieks and billyclub sweeps when the
democrats fell and the war waged on and on—
come August '68 . . .

Bughouse the forgotten dowry of 19th century-outcast
immigrant intellectuals whose battles for free speech
became our initiation into unrestricted expeditions
of infidel incantations . . .

Bughouse birth of our anti-materialistic aspirations and
altruistic idealizations, of our still thriving thankfulness . . .

Bughouse, now at the fringe of myth and legend,
never lamenting its redeemable revelations totally
irreconcilable with sub-realities of TV politics
or advertising addictions . . .

Bughouse so far away now in the all-too-confident commercial
colossus, surrounding by high-rise gentrification, still
whispering to me of its historical hopes and proclamations of
enlightenment and emancipation for a waiting humanity . . . .

Car Poem

All movement—
    an accelerated drive
through avenging
        lanes
of express-speed pain,

Of covert circulation
      outdistancing headlights
    intersecting evening
into three
    congruent infinities.

When I enter
—eyeless—
When I feel the wild rush
    of vacuumed air
        into unlit isolations
where I become
    an inconsolable departure,

When I am
    night separation.

This frozen
    thin aluminum skin
remembers its unpardoned direction
its history of coast-to-coast highways
    plowing through unrecoverable space,

Of breath
lost in frantic recollections
      dividing endlessly
in mercury-vapor haze.

Name nothing
　　and there will be no
movement—
　　　　no lethal demolitions
　　　　　　on the autosense concourse
no high-velocity explorations
　　　　　　no roadside fatalities.

Name nothing
　　　and even
　　　　　the hyperpoetic reflex
　　vanishes
without trace
　　　　into the indelible darkness
　　of unfinished road.

Car Poem
(translation)

I am driving
through the three a.m. daze
of Chicago expressways
ignited by this movement
of inexact red lights
flashing through interchanges
of displaced memories.

City at the edge
of my understanding
a forgotten megalopolis
of sidewalk seductions
where banished
in an anarchy
of unexpected turns
came summer lucidity
of urban panic.

And this car
worn with rust
and transcontinental distances
of highways from Mexico
to Manhattan
rushing uncontrolled
into these headlights
into this confusion.

I can no longer speak,
this deranged machine
accelerating
recklessly
through these empty
expressway neighborhoods
beneath towering wooden tenements

that race
    into the shadows
        of night-extinction.

And those purple flares
    and deserted bonfires ahead
  along the autowrecked roadside
    forecast another danger
certain to engulf
    my last words
  if I even try
    to stop
    to call you
    for directions home.

Terravision Blues
—A version for Robert Johnson

At home that night in 1936
  inside walls creaking under
the dry approach of August storm
  under the strain of isolation—

Then listening
    through the static scattering
unsure voices
      performing the magic annihilation
of inter-city space—

And I said to myself,
    "surely out there
  some great mind will drive
    itself to the microphone,
      will explode for an instant
  out of the anarchy of Chicago,
a meteoric confession
    for these farmlands."

  So I waited,
    listened to late-hour radio.

Until coming in hypnotic pulses
    from one of those midnight
Southern negro shows
      at the far edge of the dial,
    a hellhound haunted the air waves
with frantic delta bottleneck riffs
    of a 23-year-old
          traveling master
  working his way out
        of the incinerated body
I inherited
      as a pre-dawn storm
    erupting on the seething
      bare-wire blues horizon.

The Cure

They sent you to Kentucky for the treatment
abandoned to the forest's confession for three days
red liquid sky withdrawing from your veins
preparing you for torrid summer storms
which traced across your forehead where neither
flowers nor prayers are enough protection
against screams you recognize as your own.
When you returned and Karen asked
who had you been there?
I saw you cry for the first time.
I saw you lunge out against these dry white walls
to murder the violent history you claimed.
And if this were a lie I want another so rich
as to comfort me through the three days
of silence you gave us next.

Preaching Blues

Don't call the preacher
When you want to marry,
Don't call the doctor
to restore your health,
Just call on me, babe,
When you're tired and lonesome
I'll heal you all by myself.

(Thumping guitars)

I'll feed you when you're hungry
I'll bathe you when you're weak
I'll carry you to the raging river
You'll rise up when I commence to speak.

(Thumping guitars)

I'll let you hear the way the wind blows
I'll let you smell the hot August air
I'll let you touch the magic skyglow
I'll let you see my supernatural stare.

(Thumping guitars)

So don't call no preacher
to try to save you,
Don't call no doctor
to sell you health,
Just call on me, babe,
When you're quickly fading,
I'll give you faith all by myself.

(Thumping guitars)

I'll let you walk on golden waters
I'll lead you through the starry sky
W e'll fill fields with magic love songs
An untouched world will heed our cries.

(Thumping guitars)

So don't call no preacher
for false religions
Don't call no banker
for material wealth
Just call on me, friend,
When you're so uncertain,
I'll love you all by myself.

(Thumping guitars)

Lady of Lake Chi-Chi-c-ago

Yes it is May
and the dogwoods bless white as a sacred robe worn in Spring
and the god-lulled sun
draws forth each living molecule in melodic triumph
through the way of wind-spun maple seeds
half propellered along warm thermal updrafts
and fresh-washed corridors that escort aromatic seductions
making my eyes swell and crack with satisfaction
like I know a secret that is known to all who wish to know it
who explore geometric necessities of existence
accept only formulae coding totalities of beauty
experienced like the dull shimmer of a hazy midafternoon
so perhaps that is why she appears now
on the waters of the great lake where I am swimming
in a time before the white man or the black man wandered
where I wade alone because I live in solitude on these shores
at this moment because no one else cares to look or see
when she appears in shades even more magnificent
than the glory of sun and silver fluid substance
so that all cosmic elegance is background to her mysteriousness
her mastery of universal forces
tamed and perfected to be here now alone and supreme
upon the surface of earth they so often call blue
waiting for tribes and empires, explorers and builders
to appear and disappear
as she does when I turn so slightly.

Oh Stream of Consciousness

Oh Stream of Consciousness
Oh Stream of Consciousness
Oh Stream of Consciousness
We Kissed
                In the Morning
Of Existence

Utopian Now

uuu
tttttttttttttttttttttttt
oooooooooooooooo
ppppppppppppppppp
iiiiiiiiii
aaaaaaa
nn

nn
ooooooo
wwwwwwwwwww

ppppppppppppppppppppppp
oooooooooo
ssss
tt
u
llll
aa
tttttttttttttttttttttttt
eeeeeeeee
sssssssssssss

aaaa
aaaa
aaaa
aaaa

wwwwwwwww
hhhhhhhhhhhhh
iiii
ss
ppppppppppppppppppppp
eeeeeeeee
rrrrrr

aaaa
nn
dddddddddd

aa
aa

kkkkkkkkkkkkkkkkkkkkkkkkk
iiiiiiiiiiii
sssssssssssssssssssssss
sssssssss

What's it all about??

Shooting stars!!!

Third Eye

...,... though the eye cannot see, it is not blinded.
zoroastroistic metamorphosis of inner layers surveying
conquests of sand ... because the cat will not venture
beyond its lunar shadow.

...,.... though the eye cannot see, it is not sympathetic.
temporalizing what you think to think, what you fear to
fear, like crying all these nights and then into the dawn's
fragile awakening.

.,..... though the eye cannot see, it yields not a sickness
but a miracle. fleeing, fleeing further into its recesses
of harmonious allegations where you became a pilgrim of
love. with this kiss and another.

....., though the eye cannot see, it will still be abrupt.
supplying a cortege of salamanders swimming in pink fluid
liquid lungs. which when you dare to breathe, washes in
the truth. moments of nothingness.

....,.. though the eye cannot see, it is apt to believe
what i tell it. obedience to all soothsayers, allegiance
to unspoken prophesies and all other discursive languages
which follow obedience to the self.

                   though this yearning nets itself in tree
limbs fallen against the current of river
                   spring and autumn still pass through.

flowing outside of counting. flowing outside of time.
          flesh of sense tuned to the moving eye.

...,... though the eye cannot see, i advise you to wear it
on the outside wall of your forehead so that when these seasons
come with static storms you will not tumble lost in its numb

fragrance nor seek to devour the sheets of the cocoon which is
burying you.

.....,. though the eye cannot see, it knows more than it could
see if it could, more than it could feel, more than it will
ever say ....

Hermit

And now
as his eclectic vision
needled the windowsill eye
phantom of still another season
where from his porch lookout chair
brown like the commonwealth of forest
he could choose almost at will
his existence in imagination
ice-green sheet of northern pike skin
or the summersmile hooting owl
red tail hawk or white tail buck
phasing speed and sequence in seconds
linked with exacting visualization
transforming his location
in the timeweb of pre-human action
which warmed his hands and thighs
outside there where he was sitting
inside here where he was at last
alive

Escaped Mythologies
Episode 7877

Neon, Krypton, Xenon, all isolated in England in 1897
    by sir william ramsay
whereupon heinrich geissler invented sealedglasstube
    for examining electrocurrenting passage.
dr macfarlen moore (newark, new jersey) realized
    THE COMMERCIAL VALUE
                 of course.
then in Paris' grande palace pyramid when georges
claude exhibited the first neon signs
    no one dared think
to patent illuminating spark dischargeflow of free
electron ionized gas whose excited
                A-TOMS fueled out
light in photon quantums
          religiously,
nor discover the pink discharge signified a gas
    mostly air
        or the organicvapors the bluish grey.!!.
not until after the anacin slowdown did top professionals
print melodramatic insomnia upon the massmindlesses
of soap operatics or the offices. not once was there
human sacrifice against it until all stood neon.

neon in the livingroomsofa on the greenvelvet tuxedo
neon in the bathroomsoapdish on the pantryshelf
neon in the classwarfareroom religioussanctuary
        aviaries and insectresthomes
neon in the congressional advertisement sportsroomshelter
neon neon neon neon neon neon neon neon neon neon neon
neon neon neon neon neon neon neon neon neon neon neon

not until after the General Speculative Inversion where
the universal washout was reversed in a topological dodge
to avoid the irreconcilable did the invention of neon
disappear from the Charters Travelgraphique to permit
the respectable collapse of the Commercial Classical Empire
for the fantastic resolutions following.

Amphibian Dreams

sliding through the soft silt of underworld
          each cage
                    a rhythm to master
     for the subterranean
                    water falls
                         so deep
                         so clear
               that coral magic flares up
  in the imagination of this lizard.
serpent.
               savior.
                         snake walk of fire sermon.
listen to the underwater current seep
                    out to the deeper sea of dreams.
          listen to her scream.

Voyager

You reach this island without machines to entrap you
I have tasted the salt on your sunstroked breasts
But do not comprehend the open secret of your arrival
The photographers think you are still in New York City
I watch your face evaporate in the reflection of bonfires
Florescent nightwaves fan gardens of stars inside our eyelids
While your opulent fables forecast escapades of tranquility
Reaching for the next vista of comprehension and compassion
Where our radiant romances yield to midnight enlightenment.

Memory 1

there is neither light
nor dark
what is seen—
the succession of inexact landscapes

neither light nor dark
but the quivering exposure of streetlights
the waxed sallow-green of elm leaves
filtering electric filament

what is seen—
the succession of unsteady landforms
incessant successions
though I am not blinking
these successions.

Memory 2

almost like an illusion
or weightless vision—
it is so late
that when through the pre-dawn haze you appear
I am unprepared
to accept it—
the thin elusive movement
from the dirt alleys
which sew these dilapidated wood frames
into a town,
is your movement.

Memory 3

and I am moving too—
in such a way that visual sequence
becomes repetitive
merges—
in such a way I move
that we meet
are exposed on a corner
beneath the pale limbo of curled streetlights.

Poem Proceeding From Three Memories

you are so drunk
when at last we meet
that I think the glass glaze
of your unhealed eyes
refuses to recognize me—
until your damp hands clasp at the bridge of my neck
as you lunge
to tear me apart
with your first honest tears.

Sailing out of Byzantium

On a journey over the sea of her sickness, it was not
madness but fever that stopped us from reaching Tibet.
Instead we lived in Byzantium trading poems for
waterpipes and red Turkish rugs woven centuries ago.
Each evening benefactors from private treasuries invited
us to their feasts in search of some sign of her favor.
Great wealth lay at her fingertips, but disgusted and
distressed her like a famine. Soon we tired of reciting
ultra-contemporary quatrains of mythological enchantment
and were offended by their hatred of Sappho and Pindar,
so we broke off and survived on olives and nectar
brought in from the countryside and fish we caught from
the Bosporus and wine offered up from the cold cellars
of old men who huddled in underground bazaars where Asia
and Athens collided. We slept on the enormous rooftop of
the Sultan's Golden Crescent Hotel under a sliced canvas
tarp that let in the zodiac over-reaching an Alexandrian
Empire from which she descended into my embrace. From a
comet stream above we learned the contours of sustained
contemplation, broken each hour by fights among warring
tribal remanents in blue jeans of pillaging thieves and
smugglers whose wares lit up the tent-top with hashish
volcano roars from giant cigarettes hurled across the
pilgrimage of weary and frightened cosmopolitan
travelers venturing from Amsterdam to New Delhi
congregated there for shelter. "Where are you going?"
they asked her always in French, "May we come along?"
She smiled so slyly, "Heaven and soon, and as you wish."
On the second night of the hottest month, her self-
induced burning began, her face inflamed, her disheveled
hair scorched the silk pillow, her muscles flinching and
aching and swelling, her murmur too lenient to be heard
by any but I. And the love-sick doctors came and left
shaking their heads. So I wrapped her in damp white

sheets and carried her out into the vigil of midnight,
through cobblestone streets only wide enough for human
pack animals and lay her down in a park beside the rain-
smoothed obelisk retrieved from Egypt in some holy war,
on a bench of black marble, where she shivered and
stared at me as though I were a pharaoh prophesying her
plague. Near to oblivion she faded through figments of
seasons she once lived so long ago, hidden and forbidden
in recesses of her censored "well" mind, migrations of
oratory coded in musical mathematical equations of
thought in tune with things that are, as they will
always be. In the lonely Minaret, she was the Caliph
with a morning song of truth. All turned toward the Blue
Mosque hearing her plea for peace. Yet only I answered
her call and lay her empty body on a sloop sailing from
the Dardanelles, dropping it into the blue-green grave
of the Mediterranean where the sizzle of her soul cooled
so slowly in Neptune's swirling and silent tomb.

Vestal Virgin

Daphne collects their souls of rainbow confessions in her
sunrise vase. Saints and starving drifters reside within her
charity for centuries, faithfully delivered each dawn to the
altars of Ionic-columned temples lining the lush hillside of olive
offerings where with a prayer she invents a mirage of powder
blue benedictions, while each living organism listens to the way
her lyre of mindstring sings so melodically. "Sorry, Mr.
Timekeeper, sandsweeper," she jests, "you've got it all wrong!
While instant historical replay endangers reckless political
chronology in the refuge of freedomistic hallucinations,
time is no hang-out for the truth-seekers."

Inside the temple, priests check Daphne's thighs high above her
lofty kneecaps. Her smooth rumors are set loose on the
trembling streets of commercial speculation. Delphic confusion
infests their abusive drives for wealth. Her face reveals greater
compassion than these feeble men can hold fast, her words as
selfless as the rustling April wind parting the young shepherd
girl's golden hair and wounded cheeks.

Stonebearded, the elder statesmen listen to her magical tales
almost convincing enough for them to sacrifice their metaphors
of ships and armies as she foretells how their cities will emerge
from these hives of primitive tongues to the priesthood of
creditcards and computer banking, its herds of daylaborers and
vagrant managers fleeing in Cadillac serfdom, the pillars of
their empire, razorblades of rasping wishes she refuses to
honor. Tethered and ravaged, she appeals to their vanity with
her song of exotic exile, her body smoldering as it consumes
itself in flames of virginal sacrifice they remain too fearful to
ever worship except in the womb of their pathetic denials.

Moon Poem

It is time for a moon poem.

Dissident CIA operatives claim
    their federalist government financed
        the Apollo Program
                to kill
moon poetry.

NEVER!

Moon poetry gleams with new horizons.
Twenty times as many sunsets each day
when you silently spin around this sapphire sphere.

Still, moon poetry cannot afford
        to become romantic,
even though the old adage
      about green cheese
    had something to it.

That leering moon has wanted to eat us
        for billions of years.

Now watch it grow!

Atomic Moonbeam Poem

Lucretius lucid on the River Po
    instigating still another explanation
for LIGHT.
    Hunting luminously breezed
        sparked waves.
    Olive branches rattling along the shoreline
        of the Imperial Capital.
Thinking, "Such a long raw Spring before
        this treaty of May midnights."
    So an oar,
    tracing concentric whirlpool passions
        on the water's mirroring cosmos
    sets loose his speculations
           again.
Still, his lover's laughter
        floating like orchids
    on the vessel's white night wake,
    invites its own approval.
Turning to yield yet another caress,
        moon invasions,
    quivering yellow undulations,
    framing almost eternally,
    rows of aqua-gold expressions,
        a lunar universal of replicas
    swimming out to intersections
    where oarmarks fill their core
        before yielding quickly
    to calm unification.
And as he lifts his gaze to search
        for the real mistress herself,
    the entire river hums
    with livid liquid vibrations,
leaving for Einstein two theories
        of luminosity

in a capsule's infinitude
    and a wave's repetition.
Though his lady cares little
    which phenomena shapes their loving
        below their confidential
            corona of celestial delight.

Moon Chime

And by a tattered screen window this summer evening,
    another child whose eyes
        unlock for a first time.

A wax world wavers and wobbles,
        assumes its first amorphous shape.

Moon chimes fill the room.

Incredible!

    Is this the palace
        from whence she has descended?

    Is this the place where she is entitled
                to roam?

Orphic Dance

When at last my lyre
        leads me beyond
    the sonar eclipse
            of the sable sun

When I touch the iridescent shapes
    of ceaseless waves
        through generational memory
where cadmium light implodes
        with an imponderable voice

        Like your empty body moving
in love which is solitude

Then in some successive escape
      whose escapade leads
           past ancient ashes blowing
    in the hysteria of dead leaves
where your skeleton rises

My mystic song of passage
    plays in your receding darkness
        like a moonbeam river
beckoning you forth

      Walk on it
        and you will be free

    Glance upon me
        and our love will vanish

Recognitions

He is a god and knows it.
That is why he waits entranced in the night glow
his rust hair tossed warm with gloss of April wind
watching the shadows of shadowish forms
stalk naked across openly believing fields of winter wheat
the moon circled clouds an endless void of echoes.
A saint pants in his brain.
A dog barks in his throat.

Singing While Drunk I Stop at the Edge of Shoe Lake

Evening flows
Red drift of summer wine
Through veins of half moon streams.
I swell upon the dampened sod shore
Wedging myself between willow branches
Tracing the scent of yellow honeysuckle
Mixed with buttermilk and walnuts.
The last song a maiden sang in the tavern
Forms again as a cold apparition
On the blue mirror of star-stroked water.
Without warning,
The thin bamboo boat of a nightfisher
Slides through pearl mist of Shoe Lake.
And I am astonished to see his catfish eyes.

Lysis

For a fifth day
we inhale radiating storms
wet to our cortex
in cloud acrobatics
riding in fitful herds
like circus actors on the run
recasting harlequin laughs
in the vanishing legend
of our lives
together.

You scream
a batcry loose
in titanic caverns
where monstrous rodents
crawl through walls
of your anxious sleep
while flood waters crash
surface lines rising inescapably
threatening this very hypothesis
which crowns you observer
with the status of
parenthesis.

And that look you gave me
just now
through the lofty cross
of cottonwood arms
casts me like a single seed
deeper into the luxurious
lysis of another
October.

Killer-Whale-on-the-Sun

That Morning
returning across thunderhead ridge, splitting wilderness
into the frozen North, the quicksilver South,
cradling the fantasies of an exhausted hunter
in elkskin and sealfur,
lugging out an expedition's unenchanted harvest
of whalebone and clamclaw.
There Below
your unclaimed cadaver stretched on the bleached rivertips
ice domes erected on the Sun-Soul's arch.
Your panic so controlled your
face fleeced white in the deep sanctuary of winter.
We search until the bones of receding snow leave us only
horse hide and cattle corps.
Next Dawn
we paint your profile with blood dye on the river's swollen
snow crests,
embankments bare to windsheets even this mask will not cover.
Praying
the Killer-Whale-on-the-Sun will again show pity
we ourselves cannot learn to show.
We pray he will shrink the river dry with hot venom
will let your spirit flee to the forest
find soil for its comfort, fire for its journey.
By Noon
reports leave us limp with news
unnamed and numberless the villages washed away
near the delta mouth.
Dark
though it is on these bleak and bitter vigils
the face I sight so high above the horizon
appears the way your affections always came
rushing us both through this turbulence
to the sea. Hunters no more.

Icefisher

She fled to the hem of Ten Mile Lake which was not
Santa Barbara but certainly no longer Times Square.
Its surface blown with frozen laced flakes driving
icefishers with dogsleds deep into the vaguest shapes
of night because on the other end whispers a snowstorm
which lost them once in its wanderings. They brace
their bodies between tongues of inflammable sunrising
and wayward shapes of hemp. If the rangers trace them
they must follow alcohol flame ignited exalted on the
crystals called January. And if they track the aberrant
pulsations of their hearts on the computer map of
infrared imaginations glued to the ice's ledge, they
will decipher another verse etched in her tundra crown.
Galaxy blossoming into galaxy. And so she watched them
hunt below the ice out her front window where all
she had to do was wait by the fire for them to return.

Beaver Dam

A tune twists off Lake Winnipesaukee
               like a snake over rocks
or lizard changing seasons
         a flock of late migrating geese
filling these Elysian fields.
                    November skies releasing
the vise of expanding New Hampshire ice
               over the mud and stick dam
built by the worried beaver.
I am gathered up in the inflated arms
      of winter wind
         and sown like the initial
                         drifting of snow
      above treetops.
               Until I hear the screech
of a fleeing wood owl
deep in the forest's intoxication,
      I am afraid to cry.

Daphne Sayz

When there is nothing
to believe in,
believe in everything.

New Year

For how many births in between?
A year passing and still she
measures it in mistakes.

I want to tell her to
look at who we are another way,
brother moon
to sister sky.

"I do not believe you are a poet,
that there can be any poets."

I know what she is saying.
Sentiments we once shared.

I show her the stranded comet
in the biting 3 a.m. theatre
of the bitter winter night.

"Think of where it is going.
Of where it has been.
Now,
say who we are."

I feel a shiver rise within her,
watch its wake wash
on shores of her strained eyes.
I want to help her speak
what she feels,
but the right words will not come.

And this,
all in the first hour of the
New Year.

Rouge

An affair of roots.
Gentle man or genteel woman.
About to pursue.
Subdue.
On this stroll through the countryside.
On this promenade. On this early April day.

Like this year, like last.

Like webbing of a kite sent up over the wheat fields.
Whose motion is seasickness.
Whose spokes dance like light whistled through ice.

Together but not alone.
Treating each other to the birth of a kiss.
Above and below the oracle of forbidden desires.

Still aeons of fish skeletons are stamped in these rock.
Last year's water hyacinth shriveled.

Faradic sunsets scorch the soil
life retreating inside the earth's stomach
asking, "This much for a courtship,
                    for a civilization?"

We live in between
clean in the desert's gaze
and the sea's fist.

Like wild dry asparagus
drawn thin in a warm southerly blowing.
Slicing the lake's rimhold on a full mockingbird moon.

Blinking with seeds of the year's new warmth.
Pouches of drowsy affairs.
Of opened milkweed pods,
updrafts filled with their genetic messages.

As with tree limbs uncurling.
Time advances. Through newly shaped leaves.
Then brown musk moss covering.
With sunrising then not even its setting.
Centuries passing in the flash of one forest's concentration.

As with looking at you. Star-eyed and clairvoyant.
Lipstick stirred. About to love and be loved.
About to reveal.
About to reveal.
The sacraments of another spring.

Blue Mission

Where wind awakes Queen Anne's Lace,
Harbor mist, sundew,
Searching there for Mission Blues.

Twister

The first thunderstorms of this temperate season
thrash their way across the state like a ripsaw.
Clouds white only seconds ago flash violet
then black and swirl above with frightening fury.
Across the southwestern sky where the dark sun hides
hawks congregate in canyons of calm retreating to rain.
Squirrels scramble screeching across our rooftop.
A splitting concussion cracks the black cherry branches
flashing simultaneously with arched beam exposures
bursting above telephone poles like the ignition
of a nitrogen declaration of war while you clutch at me
as though I were a pillow escape from the ferocity
we are about to verify in an assault across the backhoed 40.
Winds descend like the metal whips of a revved-up combine
cutting unevenly through fields of twisted steel towers
with power and pitch too shrill for us to even hear
our own hoarse shrieks rising inaudible with the impact.
Tops of sweet birch snap strong and stiff like bones
busting against bats or the sides of heads slapping concrete
through the forcefall that takes a score more limbs
before piercing top soil like carelessly falling arrows.
Screen doors rip from their hinges, the windmill
flies for Florida, rear kitchen windows ring with splinters.
We dive for the basement hurled down clothes-clogged stairs.
The door behind us flips back and forth for a moment
against the frame before disappearing into throbbing
sheets of hail beating our backs like torpedo runs
as we hover within each other's quaking rib caves.
How long frozen to this tomb-filled instant I will never
remember, but when we recognize the voices
of searchers who come upon our houseless foundation
and we climb from the opened catacomb to see a blank horizon
emptied of barns and silos, we can not stop trembling.

May Pole

Pyromanic thaw.
Squill under rows of garden sleet.
Five months long.
Now lily fingers play an octave sky.
White gloves for a tuxedo day.
You the young innocent.
Burning in the arms of Erato.

Deer
Run

fawn lounge
    in your imagination
amidst vapors
      free in a focus
of sunfuse and fern
   forest and fantasy

traces you still show
     of our embraces
  inconcealable pleasures
lining your membrane language
    of unforgettable interiors

i this near to you
 inhaling rims of your water
sanity
    running supernatural rapids
 of your nocturnal
      nerve endings

Psalm 878

Always she was ravenous
    on late April night hunts
cotton blouse unbuttoned
    romping across ironwood hillsides
    altered by rainsweep
her face so well hidden
    under the gracious umbrella
        of unfolding catalpa leaves
under the lonesome romance
    of lavender
          and lilac.

Hospital Dream

When my windshield shattered
the scavenger pheasant flock
where Long Point Hill
tangles through that half-mile
yellow willow whisper
above the ice-laced lake
sealed in fortresses
of February snow,
the high octane machine
I wheeled toward town,
absorbed in its stereo simulation
of Debussy orchestrating
dances of fantail flakes,
woke to the impact
on fractured neckbone
and busted brainclods
splitting sorrel feathers,
slashed my ocular nerves
so the once visual world was
instantly circumvented by revised
laws of geophysical eurythmics
where I surveyed ninety-nine
simultaneous sunset seasons
over prehistoric bronze canyons,
traveled above unclouded pools
along ravines of fleet estuaries
seething with mutant organisms,
fell from the centipede cliff
chambers where I heard
solar wind songs sounding
so familiar as they escorted me
to the vast indigo ocean
abandoned and floating forever,
until I washed up on pink coral beaches
where gigantic cities
lay infested with the contagious
flamingo sleep.

Blacktop

blacktop
wet with the hum of autos
gliding on nomadic headlights
this turn floods
light on stalks
of broken corn husks
bent by blue frost
double center lines
chasing fierce formations
in the parabolic silence
of mountains ahead
where deer hide
in pinyon pine forests
these high-voltage lanterns
searching their camouflage
rain coats streaking
as they dash for cover
night after night
this run on route five
staring through
my rearview mirror
for the stain
of my own red
lights

Deluge

All night
   the coastal storms drive us north
a bisecting nerve pulse
  plugged into the gravitational pull
     of Route 12.

   Beyond Hatteras,
       yes, some place closer to Kitty Hawk
         the tar-pitched coil of Carolina roads
hurls us into the night's snarling serpent torch,
   lightning bails
           juggled like halos
in the godlife
      of ocean fury
        and Karmic dance.

   Your pantheon of sacred faces
    flushed full in the negative after-glow.

We see the Sivac prancers
 spinning on collapsing sandstone cliffs
  above archaic rows of Australian fir
    hovering on the curl of concrete curve
     which tosses us 360 degrees
   at the speed of regret
     toward the aquatic abyss
   until our black steel Jaguar
    buries itself in sand
and sets us loose
      bruised but bloodless.

   We stagger from its wounded carcass
crawl on the beach to the hip moan
   of the sea's violent love fantasies
    reach out for salvation
   from the steady crash
of wave pulling wave

               our bodies replying with
                              a desire of their own.

I follow you across the deserted dune trails
  twisted with clumps of long Indian grass
     and lichen-fed rock
                    russet
                         and verdant.

Your long fingers needle their way to my spine
  pulling torn fibers of nerves
                    which shape my ambitions.
          Your cure is instant
      your remedy just what I had in mind
  for moments of such demolition.

          At last the storms overtake us.
       We shiver in the tropical rain spray.
      Our bodies collide and cling,
                    reside
                         in the hush that follows.

  I see a new sun about to arise
                    in the eager eyes you show me.

  Your dawn is a rose pale sea,
          a skin of satisfied diamond lust.

     Your palms,
        like lapping white caps
                    chase the morning coastline
             where we lay
                    like beached timber washed ashore
             with water markings
      of a long
                    and untraceable journey.

Warning

Outside the cave
Of other minds
Memories loiter
Like radio transmissions
On the highway's spine
The troopers warn me
Death is the only speed trap
This side of Tulsa

Lost

Always passing in whiteouts
on lanes sewn inside the lake's frontier
where ice mosaics moan for more lovers
lonely while gearboxes expand warm liquid jaws
ice gloss spinning off pavement spills
yellow lines tied to the ignition of autoflame
while the wailer's deathswim woven
into the gigantic cordiality of snow siege
drifting like expeditions lost at the arctic core

above two deer watch starving on frost formations
as the blue metal frame sinks dark in unfed waters

Destination

Our boat bent and bound
and machete cut
with Savannah vines
twenty feet long
three feet narrow
like an African fan
cooling the lime skin of river
with eddys
of hazardous digressions
which we follow
so willingly
below the overhanging gardens
of ripening fruit
flooding our brainstorms
with esculent sensations
that leave us immobilized
as we rush into the center
of the hushed region
called Iotaxa
by those
who have hesitated
here too long
disoriented in the humming
heat of swollen flesh
and consuming adoration.
Still the whirlpools
of Aothia await us
where our souls jump from our skulls
to drown
in the wet maelstrom
like a compass bewildered
by its true destination
where we detect
each other's intentions
at last
calm and composed
inside the water memory
of whirlpool passions.

Cecropia

Called the moth of sorrow.
    West Indian lover.
        On bronze skin and on sand.

Flying from the mango
        to the lotus.
Where weave of our bodies
    was intricately
        cosmological harmony.

Called the butterflying rainbow.
    So sad in the winds of autumn
yielding to the blend of winter whirl.

Settling wings
    in seconds of living flesh.
Settling for thaw of evening,
    beyond dense smoke of opium dens
        sweet dew line of
          haunted wilderness.
Settling for isolation
    for lasting lucidity.

Then in the zones
    of long-enduring fables,
then in the zones of origins and omegas.
In the zones before our lives began
    where we cannot remember,
we remember.

Called the moth of sorrow,
    spinning inside diaphanous walls
    of hibernation,
    longing to fly through
some other lover's expectations.

An Untouchable Passes

It is not enough to keep her
not enough to touch or plead
throw off a blue silk scarf
or beg for merciful alms
swat another mosquito
making its holy alliance
of hot human blood
still you will miss
the way she walks the streets
crowded with untouchables
who part when she passes
like the night coffin split
by the accusation of moonlight
on a cow's unclean corpse.

Veda

A Brahman is watching us.
And we are examining him.
We will make a wish on his elephant.
He will not forgive us.
We will become his feed.
The Brahman always has his way.

Sahara

harmonic spills
chalk the shoreline
effervescent calm
where saffron canyons
yawn to let me touch
oh so simple a gesture
feeds the talismanic
saints with cumulus seeds
turning sands of this
season's exuberance
while stars revolve
through her arid
smile of festivities
where she entertains
a falling constellation
in the hour of blue
before taming
a desert song
as sleek vessels
of spider life
gather below
an opening moonbow
where a billion
fern print intricate
ocular codes
on giant cacti
and rare air invents
new zoological species
to stir nocturnal gossip
with powerful perfumes
washed in invisible canals
of ivory orchids,
she reaches across
her bedouin bedroll

to shave a sphere
of wild aroma
from sublunar caravans,
invents a curfew
to believe in,
swears she will meet me
Thursday
somewhere in the Sahara
where she still lives.

E Succubus Unum

I swear she was a Succubus
Who seduced me with her midnight kiss
Escorted me through eternal bliss
And transformed me into an Incubus.

Alba

Awake
all night with fever
swelling muscles
stamen-tightened skin

Awake
in your rocking arms
while lullabies
fold like blue cut iris

Awake
until you are too
much of me
until I am enough of you

Awake
in the steady stare
of a lover's dawn
fervent and sallow
satisfied and fertile

In Sleep a Poet Discovers the River's Source

Bambwa River
forms in moss-dew balm
of opal and amethyst
blossoms tossed throbbing
from garland-draped
limbs shivering
above the fluorescent fountain
welling up into 13
cascading waterfalls
of coruscating swirls
when the first sun gods
stroll through the
garden tabernacle
of Mount Omega

Apostle

Apple blossoms flutter
like aroused nipples
curling upward
on the waterbreast
of twilight river lust
a scent of lavender
rushes moist and full
from afternoon showers
sweeping across my flesh
gentle as the white
light heat of summer love.
Stretched out on a sofa
of mulberry and laurel
I fall far away back
to our last encounter
when your fingers
made loom of my thighs
and my eyes wove
deep with your stare
until neither of us
could see what
the other did not know.
Why did I leave
the home we built
to follow this river
try to fathom
its silent turnings
while you crumpled
like a neglected child
sick with fear and fever
that burnt our village
so I could not return
my last adoration spread
like hot dry ashes
across the grave
of an angry night

where nothing was forgotten?
Now I skim my hands
across water's famished face
looking for your reflection
grasping for your inviting
thighs your quivering lips
my arms rippling through foam
that leaves no trace
knowing how far
I have traveled
to master nothing
once love was abandoned.

Asylum

I enter your asylum of artistic lies
beyond the isle of lost taboos
where idols of fire pillars
whistle crackling incantations
like a seasonal siren
beating sheets of flaming masks
against dark thunderheads
flashing above chalk-white cliffs
where you move like the whip of a willow
in an imperceptible wind
teaching the holy men the difference
between charity
and conceit
fable and fiction
victory and vanity
while I follow your fantasy of sleep
where you slip away
to the kingdom
of sensual intoxications.

Blue Divan

I have heard the Scribes disclose how they were ushered
into gilded council chambers deep in the Ottoman Empire
to recite a single sacred sound like a solemn god pearl
offered from the satin pillow of their royal tongues.

Instead I laid on the blue divan beside Sultan's first bride
as inextricable as a dynasty of incandescent desert nights
raging beyond the contours of Pasha's pink marble palace
while she filled me with more poems than I could decipher.

Hard Advice

I told her to tell the time that night
between mid-moon and pale twilight
when apartments go black from white
and snow seals the streets ice tight
a void avoiding human sight.

I told her to stay up until the dawn
sprawled out across the frozen lawn
to sing its low and lazy song
for her temptations so long gone
passing like her casual yawn.

I told her to think it through all alone
in the distance of her brilliant dome
expanding through that forbidden zone
of the white and hazy foam until
she reached her own forbidden poem.

Cosmic Chatter

"Let us assume," she confided, "that the universe
as it presents itself to the mass of minds that
come to contemplate its magnificence is but a
figment of one permissible perspective limited
by the finitude it holds within infinite
infinities of multiple realities. Then who does
not know to seek the ways of the wise ones
of ancient preconceptual days who understood fully
that the truth of this moment is absolutely held
within the spheres of eternalizing awareness?"

Conductor

Don't wait for the conductor
to throw you a kiss
when your strings snap under the strain of a high octave E
or when your bow tightens
with arrows
of broken crescendos.
His black tuxedo
turns yellow
when the audience laughs
at your new existential discovery
and he cancels the season finale
on account of feigned fatigue.
You know that kind of perfectionist
who cannot smile when his first violinist outshines him
who shatters crystal at parties
with his witty intolerance.

Solace

So time runs out.
Whatever day this was is over.
At two hours after midnight
my eyes stick to the backside of my memory
and the long blue candle flame that lingers in the corner
is like the threat of a thought that leads me to you
receding inside strange trances where we once met
like the echo of a song you sang all night
while we sought solace in fingercurves and tonguetips
that raced through our sleep to the kingdom of desire
where we found a reed so thin
it whistled in the motionless wind
waiting for silence that stirred as it began
another morning
marking its departure deep in our darkness.

(Ergo) Sumus

Here I think I am again.
There are three of me today.
And so I ask us why they
have gathered without greetings.
Each is ashamed to answer.
Bonescrap, heartbulge, nervetwist, tongue.
Each is afraid to question.
And so I ask us why they
have gathered without speaking.
There are nine of me today.
Here I think I am again.

Standard Time

Ten minutes pass.
I write a decade of verse.
Each
            featherfalls
outside of thinking time.
BeYond
the constant Cesium pulse
synchronized
at 9,192,631,770 beats
                        per second.
Word by word
        spark by quark
        I swim alone
        in dislocated tides
                of ion river flame
        seeking the remote
                dark shore
                of the Hineyana.

Daphne Thinks Again

Once while following the roll of Fawn River
to a grove of cloud white dogwood blossoms
Daphne thought to herself, "Since it is such
a superficiality, TIME can never be wasted."

Lemma
33

My alphabetic acrobatics land on unaccented feet.
Fig trees grow in golden fields of my imagination.
Striving for images to shoot at the swollen sun,
I have forgotten to check my own vest pocket.
A thousand black and orange butterflies escape.
I eat the caterpillar that crawls out last.
Slumber invades my anguished body and flutters.
I awaken in someone else's overcoat pocket.
When she checks for a match to light her tunnel,
Scattered pages of poems choke the night sky.
But she is bored by unpopular literature.
Swats my similes like winter flies on her windowsill.

Lady at the Window

Snow gardener
You tend to rose skulls
half-buried in windsung ice drift
red and yellow shells stranded on whitened soil
their tongues climbing your trellis of wooden legs
and weakened arms planted
inside double cherry doors of bevelled glass
where you survey the geometry
of measured walkways circumventing
Japanese miniature trees and Shinto shrines
under winter's slow dull sun dial
circling your arctic oasis
till the lantern gaze
of January moonrise
becomes phantom night falling
in your heart of shattered lovers.
Your face flushes with blood of frozen rose death.
Your body endures a cold more primeval than snow.

The History of Religion

Episode 7

The Buddha Is
Concentrating
on his
(word censored by Congressional/NEA mandate),
the long drawn out syllogism
from whence his
"First Great Truth"
"All Is
Suffering,"
origin-all-y
came.

First Impressions

When first I saw you among the chrysanthemums
I thought you were a secret gardener.

When next I encountered you in the atrium's turquoise pool
I took you for a golden fish with a penny's wish.

But now that I meet you in my inner sanctum
I wonder if you really are a chambermaid
ready to change my disposition.

Share My Shades

Why don't you come on and share my shades,
baby, won't you share my shades,
got so hot outside we can't see the sun,
so honey won't you share my shades?

You know it's high high noon,
we're sweating too soon,
we're blind as spring lovers,
we got to dive for cover,
so come on and share my shades.

They got red rose frames,
they got cold black glass,
they got fancy hinges and rims of brass,
they got X-Ray Vision,
they got Z-Ray Feel,
they got cosmic sight,
they got Sex-Appeal.

So why not share these shades, my friend,
why not share my shades,
let's dive inside,
put the air conditioner on,
and baby, let me pull down my shades.

I Wake in an Unfamiliar Field after Hitch-Hiking All Night

Like broken shale soil
my chest springs a florid pasture
lush with labial peonies
34 white cream
14 pious pink prayers
stemless layers
of petalskin
lathering my graveyard
of bone wanderings
as though calling for an armistice.

Beauty on the Beach

Beauty built her fine
fine shine
on her blonde blonde
baby blueblood back
her rich tan span
of sand-stretched thighs
where lie about her
lavishly a plumage
of patriarchal peacocks
and papyrus-eating pandas
disguised as high-salaried
suitors in tight bathing suits
though she prefers sailcraft
and flying-fish fleet
for her company
on the summerfest
oceanbliss.
Beauty thought
she was
a sea sea mermaid
a free free
swimming being
born of evaporating foam
and salt-glistened spray
like daylight gambolling
on the occult glass
of watersplash
from no one knows where
singing singing
her viola vagabond vibration
stirring stirring
a spectrum of sacrosanct smiles
transcendentally traversed
until until

the sand turns to mist
and she is trapped
inside the shell
of a transient snail
splashing lashing
always her sigh
her surprise
when her real self defies
beginning or end
the sound she is
laughs itself loose again.

Hysteria

So I asked her why she screamed at the sea.
And she showed me her body
of empty shells and endless sand.

Summer Solstices

Sunset in some small town backyard wild with hollyhocks and
iris and towering oaks slowly twisting in the hot June wind.
The low second story arch of a Coolidge cabin decked out in
yellow with thin white trim and limestone cubed blocks from
the swimming quarries and the backsteps that stand before the
lattice low across the foundation where wild roses yellow, pink
and red crawl and cling. Lilacs creep to the screen porch
rooftop next to a hidden garden of abandoned tomatoes,
onions and asparagus greens. In the one hundred degrees of
this afternoon the distant fields bake like potatoes in the blast
of heat from the panhandle that hits like an oven opened on a
baby's face. The dogs pant like hunted rabbits but I am not too
listless to move to spray them down with the hose then escape
to the university pool where fahrenheit blue chlorine lanes hide
the sorority beauty queens wet to their necks in the naked
water where cool still sizzles and their thoughts turn so slowly
like the roast on a backyard barbecue that takes hours to finish
as they will takes hours to complete in the heat of the night
which will follow this worship of light. By six o'clock the
scorcher tunes down to 93 on the city square where the art fair
draws crowds of hundreds standing in stifling lines to be fed
like angry hogs grunting and kicking against their fences. After
the fifth shower of the day we retreat again to the backyard to
watch the stars turn up beyond the wisp of blue imperishable
sky. In light buff pinstripes and soft white cotton shirt over the
pink burnt skin of these shoulders I am ready for the
wedding feast that will wish a lifetime romance while I really
wonder how far the sun has run from us as the plains fill with
thin mist and the open hillsides cradle the cry of the new born
moon in the somnolent shelter of fog. Waves of orange halos
magnify the light around my cupped hands which circulate like
fireflies and all is mystique and so complete so absolute and
perfected. Day of the longest light, this night which is the
shortest is certainly the most blessed by beauty. Hazel aqua
thrills the chill that is oh so deep and still. Sky the cream of sea
of dream divided into unequal totalities. If waking now or
sleeping is the end, then this day will always be what yet begins.

Sideshow

Dear doctor of dramatic sublimations,
listen, tonight is another performance
in the Age of Post-Freudian Frigidity
in the Epoch of Extravagance and Suicide,
calm the national audience before it expires
or decimates Earth with another random invention,
tell them to stand watch above the coastline at dawn.
From a beggar's tin cup I'll empty an incarnadine ocean,
flood the emerald sky with specks of living flesh,
lost stars I'll pick from their seasick eye sockets
like cards from the oracle's ancient stacked deck,
showing the Republic 54 ways to split infinity.

Charmer

You read the fluorescent diamond letters
vanished language magic scrawl
coded on the black snake's cold earth skin
coiling through your frantic field of strawberry hair
his tongue quick on the crest of your rising breasts.
Once before he was your lover.
His skinwords singed your flesh already tattooed
with exotic lore of romantic excavations.
Once you were his victim. His dreamdomain.
His eyes of silver film sharpen for the tonguesting.
For the master's lust. For the religious kill.
But this time you neglect him. Punish him
with exile among the reptile calls
swelling in the insect forest flood of summerheat.
Your sacred spin of spiderlives lace together
fir and pine and shoreline of skyscroll
its web of sunspray stretching to the recoiling quilt
of silk stored in the pillow behind your dust red eyes.
You lift your flute of carved Acacia.
A song begins from everywhere.
You call it dancing, dancing across the stardust.
You call it your Edenworld.
It was there you first charmed me.

Lagoon

We glide on a lagoon where willows
go limp with slumber—
where the whitefish twilight yawns.

Where psalms sweep the fleet of swan
through magnolia dusk—
circle swirls of moonworked water.

Oars feather the glassy eye of night
with a midstream thaw—
night perspires a nuclear mist.

Aurora's awakening lilies
whose vision we hunt—
bloom in the galactic garden.

Like drunken nightfishers we chase
bruised splashes to the sea-sound's source.

We are the harvest of flesh and stars
yielding more than the earth can bear.

PRB

Afloat on the daydreaming lotus.
A river of hypnotic laudanum below your pulse
overdosed and satisfied Lizzy you call out
and the wind of swaying willow songs replies.
Your long smooth body of hidden flesh,
like scarves of gossamer veil, reclines on cool
rafts of honey stream, sweet and tasty, stirred
and scented with sage paregoric sighs.
Who is to be your lover in death?
Rossetti who neglected you? Bourne-Jones or
Millais who painted you? Your counselor,
the benevolent, wise and impotent Ruskin?
Your arms are rows of floating hyacinth too weak
to hold even your own life of suffering and beauty.
Those faces below the dark languid surface
are the suspended wishes of water lilies.
The organ chords you hear are the lavish laughter
of your empty hands dipping under the rippled sap
to anoint your captives with ointments of mercy.
You are but an obscure idol in the Brotherhood's
Pre-Raphaelitic gallery, the oiled vision of Ophelia
taunted by half-tone sacrifices and delusions,
the sensuous muse of their medieval immortalities.
Your limbs of narcissine episodes float to the surface.
Your dress fills the sunspun river like a gondola.
Your hundred heads of streaming strawberry hair spin
metamorphosized epiphanies to the melodic mandala
clasp like a ruby in the teeth of watching demi-gods.
Lizzy, not only the gallery of tin critics listen
when you chant, "Master, master, birds are lost frogs,
spiders are starstruck moths, and you, you my love,
are still the question the breeze stutters
when dusk divides twilight into an unalterable signature
of lonely poets and abandoned models afraid to move,
and I no more than your symbolic imitation of morality."
Lizzy, we all hear your body sinking in sightless silt.
"Blame it on the moonman signing PRB," you told us,
"that exquisite thief, that deadly lord."

Gamehouse

With quivering nerves and loss of eyesight
spaceship, computer track, a pong bounce
away from the neon pulsating gamehouse
soundprinted with Sonny Boy Williamson's
blues-pitched sonar wail
and ten-hole matchbox.
Outside the club, he huddled below
the five-hundred-foot factory wall hollow
whose graffiti glowed pale purple
when the winter moon passed over.
All he owned,
spread out with his vacant arms
offering an allegiance
to the distant nebular sirens
whose secret explorers
haunt the earth on crescent midnights,
reminding him of his theory
that all these voices surrounding him
were nothing but phantom transmissions
of light year missionaries
expanding through super-conscious space,
their exquisitely crafted bodies
contrived as poetic illuminations
of matching worlds
which we plunder so heedlessly.
And in this arcade of reconciliation,
love had to mean,
what he had always wanted it to mean,
an all-protecting cosmic sympathy
whose outermost sphere we were fast becoming,
in spite of how we still tormented ourselves.
And for this magic,
he was willing enough to breathe in the sky,
to release it as a temple
in which he would now sleep.

Quantum theories of atomic processes proposed
by Neils Bohr in 1913, based upon earlier
models of Rutherford, were not very comforting
in bed. Even so, the Reibergian number for
Universal Atomic Constants was its first
convincing confirmation, giving birth to Bohr's
theorem as a compromise between classical Newtonian
propositions and the new quantum physics of Max Planck.
Quantums lit up the island of escaped isotopes
around the region of Van Gogh's asylum several
years before, but formal science was not ready
to credit the insane with this structural discovery.
From then on, picture failures of space and time
were documented in the history of French cinema
where the new stage of false coordinates reversed
with precise numbering of anti-material window markings
of the next interminable medium and matrix.
Statesmen gathered in for the headliners.
The General spoke before reporters and bellowed,
"Our generation has witnessed physical knowledge before,
but it scarcely compares to the new breakthroughs.
Consider the importance of removing ourselves
from the future!" "Marvelous" was the cry of the epoch.
"We will make history inaccessible as well!"
chimed the Senatorious. "Splendid."
One group of rotations in a nine-dimensional space
affirmed the unity of vector analysis in unordered
calculus. These laws were as holy as any subspace
communicative system. Mapping space "K" for example,
every emotion of the survivors became derivative to
the last incident in the series. So what was thought
to be cause was somewhere result, the future past,
memory, prophecy, etc, cte.
As the history of science became more reprehensible,

new discoveries multiplied. The initial calculation
for void "E," stood in oppositional logical time
of high physical concentration. Science, as a result
of this miscalculation, was reduced to the shadow
vibrations of three unknown Mississippi poets whose
lives spanned four centuries and one work. In the
retranslated zones of commerce it was all too shocking.
Underground laboratory complexes burst out in
uncontrollable laser rotations. The general disintegration
of civilization quickly followed and the star burnt out.
All three poets momentarily put down their pens
and drew in a new harmonic tone before beginning again.

Evolution

Diners at the apocalyptic revelation
raven and kingmaker
sword follower and priest.

The dragon's eye fires
the fish's swirl
the coyote's howl
the teacher's scowl.

When avenging flights of self-persecution
twist in the lunar gales.

Along the tangerine-green mercury stream
at twilight where we disrobe our sins,
swim naked in the cooling schism of confession.

But why, you ask,
is this evolutionary expedition
so savage?
The biological hierarchy so cruel?

Whose interpretation will follow
the skeletal path
built on our glass foundations
magnificent
in their
grand delusions?

Listen. I tell you,
from this brutality,
some higher beauty
will spiral.